TELL THE TRUTH, GRUMPY BUNNY!

To Roy Wandelmaier and everybunny else
who struggles to stay solid in a hollow world.
—J.K.F.

In memory of our sweet brother and sister, Vincie and Alice.
—Lucy

Text copyright © 2008 by Justine Korman Fontes
Illustrations copyright © 2008 by Lucinda McQueen

All rights reserved. Published by Scholastic Inc.
SCHOLASTIC, GRUMPY BUNNY, and associated logos are trademarks
and/or registered trademarks of Scholastic Inc.

ISBN-13: 978-0-439-02011-4
ISBN-10: 0-439-02011-5

12 11 10 9 8 7 6 5 4 3 2   8 9 10 11 12 13/0

Printed in the U.S.A.
First printing, March 2008

TELL THE TRUTH, GRUMPY BUNNY!

by Justine Korman Fontes
Illustrated by Lucinda McQueen

SCHOLASTIC INC.

New York   Toronto   London   Auckland   Sydney
Mexico City   New Delhi   Hong Kong   Buenos Aires

Chapter 1
Little Bunny, Big Mouth

Hopper sometimes stretched the truth
to make his stories more exciting.
He told his friends, "I caught a fish as
big as our boat!"
"Where's the fish?" Corny asked.
"We had to throw it back—or sink,"
Hopper said.
"Wow!" Corny exclaimed.
And Hopper smiled.
He liked when his friends said "Wow!"

One day, everybunny was talking about chocolate.

"My family always buys Solid-Chocolate Bunnies," Hopper said.

Corny didn't quite hear. "Did you say your family knows The Solid-Chocolate Bunny?"

Hopper couldn't help himself.
He began another story. "Dad worked
with him in the city," he said.

Suddenly everybunny was listening
and asking questions.
"What's he like?"
"What's his real name?"
"Is he really tall, dark, and honest?"

Hopper loved all the attention.
And his lie seemed harmless.
Until…

...Sir Byron, the principal, said, "Then Hopper must already know my surprise."
Hopper's ears tingled.
"The Solid-Chocolate Bunny himself will be at school tomorrow," Sir Byron said.

Everybunny cheered!
But Hopper's stomach sank.
Tomorrow everybunny would find out that his story wasn't true!

Chapter 2
A Very Dark Night

Hopper didn't know what to do.
Should he pretend to be sick and stay
home from school?

Then Hopper heard Marigold talking to
Lilac. "Do you think Hopper really knows
The Solid-Chocolate Bunny?"
Lilac giggled. "Can he catch a fish as big
as a boat?"

That night, Hopper couldn't fall asleep.
So he made a wish on a star.
Hopper wished that he could stop
telling lies.
He wished that his friends would still
like him.
And that somehow everything would
work out.

Finally, Hopper fell asleep.
But his dreams were all a jumble.
In one, Hopper was being chased by
an army of angry chocolate bunnies!

In another, Hopper was caught by a
giant fish!
"Let me go! Let me go!" Hopper cried.
But the fish just laughed.

The next morning, Hopper was very tired
and very grumpy.
He could barely brush his teeth.
Hopper dragged his feet to the bus stop.
He was just in time—to miss the bus!
"Oh, worms!" Hopper cried. "Now I'll
have to walk to school."

Chapter 3
Fast Friends

Soon Hopper saw someone on the
path ahead.
The someone was tall and dark.
Could it be?
Hopper ran ahead to see.
It was.
"The Solid-Chocolate Bunny!"
Hopper cried.

"In the fur," the big bunny replied.
"Actually, my name is Felix Moss."
He shook Hopper's paw. "I hope we
can be friends."
Hopper's paw felt lost in warm fur.
*I hope it happens before we get to
school*, he thought.

Just as Hopper hoped, the two became
friends.
The Solid-Chocolate Bunny tested his
speech on Hopper.

"When I was young, I bit a hollow, fake-chocolate bunny. Did I like it?" Hopper shook his head. "No, sir!"

REAL and SOLID CHOCOLATE

MEADOW MONTHLY

BUNNY OF THE YEAR

FELIX MOSS

SOLID + REAL

Before long, their sunny walk was over.
Sir Byron himself came out to greet them.
"Welcome!" he said.

Then he saw Hopper and added,
"Why don't we let your old friend
Hopper introduce you?"
Hopper could hardly believe his good luck.
His story was turning true!
If only Mr. Moss would go along with it.

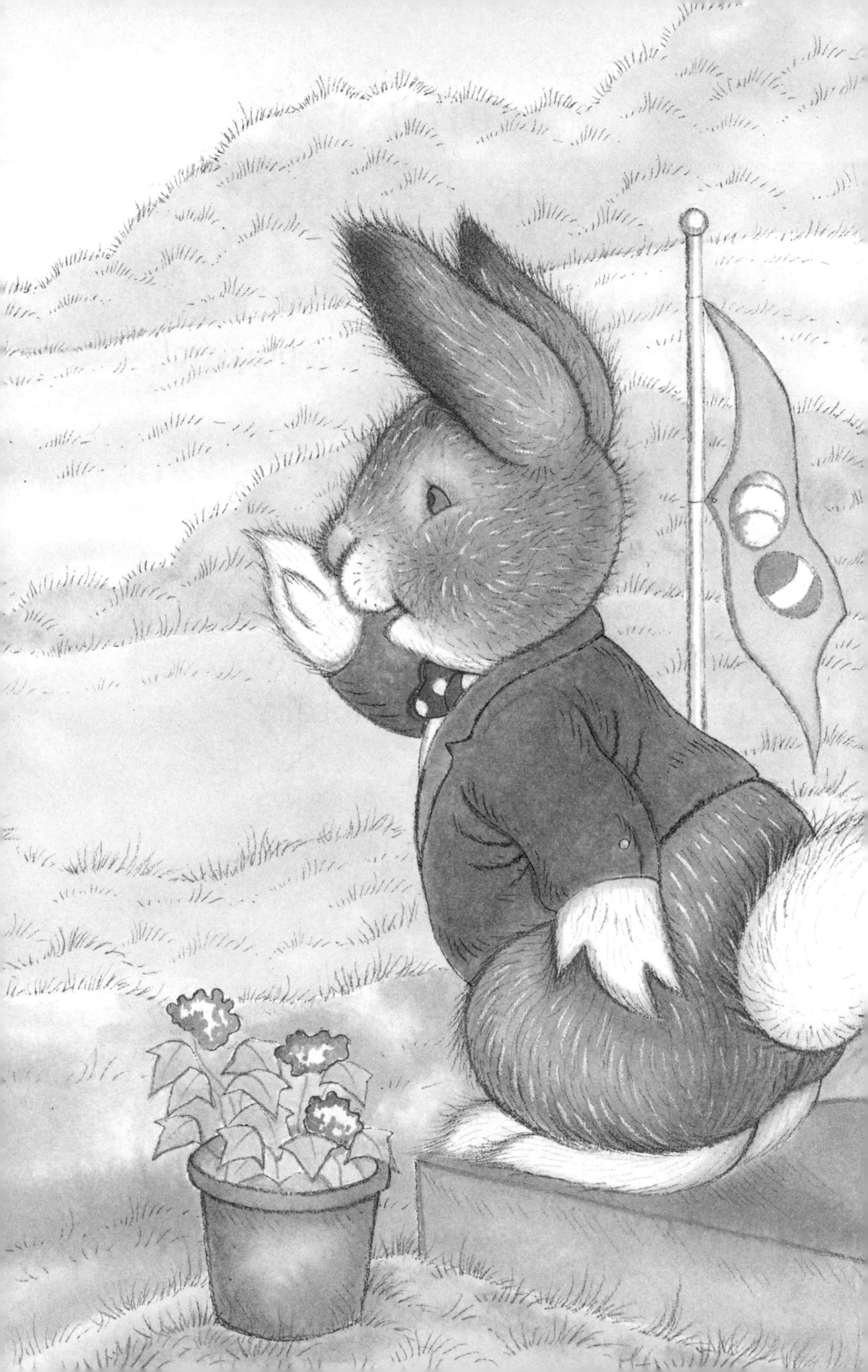

Chapter 4
One Last Lie

"That would be grand!" Felix agreed.
Hopper whispered, "Please don't tell
anyone we just met."
It was time to go on.

Hopper said, "I'd like you all to meet
my good friend, Felix Moss, also known
as The Solid-Chocolate Bunny."
Everybunny cheered, "Hooray!"

Hopper felt happy—until the end of
Mr. Moss's speech.
Felix thanked Sir Byron and his new
friend Hopper O'Hare.
"Even though we only met this morning,
I'm sure we'll be great friends,"
The Solid-Chocolate Bunny said.

Everybunny burst out laughing.
Hopper blushed red and he felt
like crying.

Hopper felt someone's paw tap his
shoulder.

Lilac whispered, "Don't cry."

Then Corny clapped Hopper on the back.

"Tell us how you really met Mr. Moss."

Hopper smiled. "Well, I missed the bus
this morning and…"

"…took the same flying saucer as The
Solid-Chocolate Bunny?" Marigold teased.

Lilac laughed. "It's okay, Hopper. We like your silly stories."

"Yeah," Corny agreed. "But we like to hear the truth, too."

So Hopper told the story exactly as it happened.

And Corny said, "Wow!" anyway.

Later, Mr. Moss said, "Hopper, you're too nice a bunny to fall into bad habits. Tell the truth and everybunny will love you. I promise."
Of course, Hopper believed him.
He felt solid and warm inside.
Hopper told the truth from that day on.